CONJURE TALES

CONJURE TALES

by Charles W. Chesnutt
retold by
Ray Anthony Shepard

illustrated by John Ross
and Clare Romano

E. P. DUTTON & CO., INC.
New York

Introduction and Retelling copyright © 1973
by Ray Anthony Shepard

Illustrations copyright © 1973 by John Ross
and Clare Romano Ross

LIBRARY OF CONGRESS CATALOGING IN PUBLICATION DATA

Shepard, Ray Anthony.   Conjure tales.

CONTENTS: The goophered grapevine.—Poor Sandy.—
Master James' nightmare. [etc.]

1. Magic—Juvenile fiction.   1. Magic—Fiction.
2. Slavery in the United States—Fiction.
3. Short stories   I. Chesnutt, Charles Waddell,
1858–1932. The conjure woman.   II. Romano, Clare,
illus.   III. Ross, John, 1921–   illus.   IV. Title.

PZ7.S5432Co   [Fic]   73-77457   ISBN 0-525-28140-1

Published simultaneously in Canada by Clarke,
Irwin & Company Limited, Toronto and Vancouver

Designed by Riki Levinson
Printed in the U.S.A.
First Edition

For Rachel, Sarah, Nathan,
and Peter Blain

INTRODUCTION

Charles Chesnutt was born in Cleveland, Ohio, in 1858, but his family moved to Fayetteville, North Carolina, when he was eight. After a few years his mother died and his father urged him to quit school to help support the family. In order to help his father and to continue his education at the same time, Chesnutt became a fourteen-year-old teacher. He continued his learning and teaching for many years and when he was twenty-two he became a school principal.

Chesnutt loved writing, but he became increasingly aware that life in North Carolina as a black man was limited, no matter how much education he had. In 1883 he moved back to Cleveland and began to study law. Chesnutt continued to write and in 1887 his short story "The Goophered Grapevine" appeared in the *Atlantic Monthly*. Following the success of this tale, he contributed other stories to the magazine. In 1899 Chesnutt's conjure stories were collected and published as a book, *The Conjure Woman*. When the stories first appeared in the *Atlantic Monthly*, his readers assumed

he was white, since his editors refused to tell them otherwise.

Between 1899 and 1905 five more books appeared. But soon it became clear that Chesnutt was a black writer. After 1905 his books became less and less successful and Chesnutt gave up writing and concentrated on being a lawyer and a businessman. He died on November 15, 1932.

This book, *Conjure Tales,* is a reworking of the 1899 book, *The Conjure Woman.* I have retold these tales because they are my favorite short stories and I wanted as many readers as possible to discover them. It seemed to me that this was a good way of introducing Charles Chesnutt and some early Afro-American writing to younger readers. These stories also reveal much about slavery, in a way that a tired old history book can never do. But most of all, they make for good reading.

The stories are set in North Carolina just before the Civil War. Chesnutt created Uncle Julius, a former slave, to tell them. Although we are never introduced to Uncle Julius in *Conjure Tales,* it is his voice that narrates the stories.

When these tales were written, many southern white authors were writing about what the South was like before the Civil War. They often showed that a slave's life was a happy and an easy one. Since most of Chesnutt's readers, in 1887, thought he was white, they failed to see how he revealed slavery to be evil and destructive. These tales can be compared in certain ways with Joel Chandler Harris' Uncle Remus tales. Harris, who lived from 1848 to 1908, adopted a slave dialect for his stories, although he was white. However, Harris' animal stories tell the reader very little about

the lives of the slave characters, and paint the happy slave picture. It is not surprising that we all know of Joel C. Harris and his Uncle Remus and only a few people know of Charles Chesnutt and his Uncle Julius.

Some readers might not know what *conjuring* means. Conjuring was brought over from Africa by the slaves. It became known as *hoodoo,* or *voodoo,* in some parts of the United States, the West Indies, and Latin America. It was the belief that certain people, called conjure doctors, had supernatural powers. They exercised these powers with the aid of roots, herbs, and many other kinds of ingredients that could be used to make a mixture. The conjure woman or man worked the roots by rubbing them in her hands, or moving the root between her fingers. Or she would make a goopher mixture, or goopher. This power was strong enough to turn Sandy into a tree, a slave master into a slave, Mahaly into a cat, and Dan into a wolf.

Another word that might be unfamiliar is *haint,* which is an early Afro-American word for haunt, spirit, or ghost. I think the reader now has enough information to enter this strange world of slavery and conjuring. And I hope these stories will be as meaningful to you as they are to me.

April 1973
Roxbury, Massachusetts   RAY ANTHONY SHEPARD

CONTENTS

Poor Sandy   1

The Conjurer's Revenge   15

The Gray Wolf's Haint   27

Master James' Nightmare   43

The Goophered Grapevine   61

Hot-Foot Hannibal   75

Sister Becky's Child   87

POOR SANDY

Sandy used to belong to old Master Marlboro. You know, the old Marlboro place on the other side of the swamp. Well, Sandy was a mighty good hand, he could do many things around the plantation. In fact, he did his work so well that when Master Marlboro's children grew up and married off, they all wanted their daddy to give them Sandy for a wedding present. But Master Marlboro knew the rest wouldn't be satisfied if he gave Sandy to just one of them. So when they were all married, Master Marlboro gave Sandy to each of his children for a month or so. When they all had him the same length of time, he was passed around again and again. Once in a while Master Marlboro would lend Sandy to some of his other kinfolks when they were shorthanded. Well, this went on until it got so Sandy didn't hardly know where he was going to stay from one week to the other.

One time when Sandy was lent out as usual, a speculator came along with alot of slaves, and Master Marlboro swapped Sandy's wife off for a new woman. When Sandy came back, Master Marlboro gave him a

dollar, and allowed he was mighty sorry to break up the family, but the speculator had given him a good offer, and times were hard and money scarce, so he was best to make the trade. Sandy took on something about losing his wife, but he soon saw it wasn't no use crying over spilt molasses. And being as he liked the looks of the new woman, he took up with her after she had been on the plantation a month or so.

Sandy and his new wife got on mighty well together, and the rest of the slaves all commenced to talk about how loving they were. When Tenie took sick once, Sandy set up all night with her, and then went to work in the morning just like he had his regular sleep, and Tenie would have done anything in the world for her Sandy.

Sandy and Tenie hadn't been living together for more than two months before Master Marlboro's old uncle, who lived down in Robinson County, sent word up if Master Marlboro couldn't let him hire him a good hand for a month or so. Sandy's master was one of these here easygoing folks who wanted to please everybody, so he says yes, he could lend him Sandy. So Master Marlboro told Sandy to get ready to go down to Robinson County the next day to stay a month or so.

It was mighty hard on Sandy to be taken away from Tenie. It was so far down to Robinson County that he didn't have no chance of coming back to see her until the time was up. He wouldn't mind coming ten or fifteen miles at night to see Tenie, but Master Marlboro's uncle's plantation was more than forty miles off. Sandy was mighty sad and cast down after what Master Marlboro told him.

He told Tenie, "I'm getting tired of this here going around so much. Here I am lent to Master James this

month, and I got to do so and so. Then to Master Archie the next month, and I got to do so and so. Then I got to go over to Miss Jenny's and it's Sandy this and Sandy that, and Sandy here and Sandy there, until it appears to me that I ain't got no home, no master, no mistress, nor no nothing. I can't even keep a wife. My other woman was sold away without my getting a chance to tell her good-bye. And now I got to go off and leave you, Tenie, and I don't know whether I'm ever going to see you again or not. I wish I was a tree, or a stump, or a rock, or something that could stay on the plantation for a while."

After Sandy got through talking, Tenie didn't say a word, but just sat there by the fire, thinking and thinking. Finally she upped and said:

"Sandy, I ain't never told you I was a conjure woman?"

Of course Sandy had never dreamed of nothing like that, and he made a great admiration when he heard what Tenie had said.

By and by, Tenie went on. "I ain't goophered nobody, nor done no conjure work, for fifteen years or more. When I got religion I made up my mind I wouldn't work no more goopher. But there are some things I don't believe it's no sin to do, and if you don't want to be sent around from pillar to post, and if you don't want to go down to Robinson County, I can fix things so you won't have to. If you'll say the word, I can turn you into whatever you want to be, and you can stay right where you want to be. And you can stay right where you want to as long as you got a mind to."

Sandy didn't care, he was willing to do anything to stay close to Tenie. So Tenie asked him if he didn't want to be turned into a rabbit.

3

Sandy said, "No, the dogs might get after me."

"Shall I turn you into a wolf?"

"No, everybody is scared of a wolf, and I don't want nobody to be scared of me."

"Shall I turn you into a mockingbird?"

"No, a hawk might catch me. I want to be turned into something that will stay in one place."

"I can turn you into a tree," said Tenie. "You wouldn't have no mouth nor ears, but I can turn you back once in a while so you could get something to eat, and hear what was going on."

"Well," said Sandy, "that'll do."

And so Tenie took him down by the swamps, not far from the slave quarters, and turned him into a big pine tree, and set him out among some other trees. The next morning, as some of the field hands were going along there, they saw a tree that they didn't remember, or else one of the saplings had been growing mighty fast.

When Master Marlboro discovered that Sandy was gone, he thought he had run away. He got the dogs out, but the last place they could track Sandy to was the foot of that pine tree. And there the dogs stood and barked and bayed and pawed at the tree, and tried to climb up on it. When they were taken around through the swamp to look for the scent, they broke loose and made for the tree again. It was the darndest thing the white folks had ever heard of, and Master Marlboro figured that Sandy must have climbed up on the tree and jumped off on a mule or something, and rode far enough to spoil the scent. Master Marlboro wanted to accuse some of the other slaves for helping Sandy run off, but they all denied it to the last and everybody knew Tenie set too much in store by Sandy

to help him run away where she couldn't never see him no more.

When Sandy had been gone long enough for folks to think he done got clean away, Tenie used to go down to the woods at night and turn him back, then they would slip up to the cabin and sit by the fire and talk. But they had to be careful, or else somebody would see them, and that would spoil the whole thing. So Tenie always turned Sandy back in the morning early, before anybody was stirring.

But Sandy didn't get along without his trials and tribulations. One day a woodpecker came along and started to peck at the tree. The next time Sandy was turned back he had a little round hole in his arm, just like a sharp stick had been stuck in it. After that, Tenie set a sparrow hawk to watch the tree, and when the woodpecker came along the next morning to finish his nest, he got gobbled up before he stuck his bill in the bark.

Another time, Master Marlboro sent a slave out in the woods to chop turpentine boxes. The man chopped a box in this here tree and hacked the bark up two or three feet, in order to let the turpentine run. The next time Sandy was turned back he had a big scar on his left leg, and it took Tenie about all night to make a mixture to fix him up. After that, Tenie set a hornet to watch the tree, and when the slave came back again to cut another box on the other side of the tree, the hornet stung him so hard that the axe slipped and cut his foot about off.

When Tenie saw so many things happening to the tree, she concluded she would have to turn Sandy to something else. And after studying the matter over, and talking with Sandy one evening, she made up her

mind to fix up a goopher mixture that would turn herself and Sandy to foxes, or something, so that they could run away and go someplace where they would be free and live like white folks.

Tenie had got the night set for her and Sandy to run away, when that very day young Master Dunkin, one of Master Marlboro's sons, rode up to the big house in his buggy and said his wife was mighty sick and he wanted his Mama to lend him a woman to nurse his wife. The mistress said to send Tenie, since she was a good nurse. Of course the young master was in a terrible hurry to get back home. Tenie said she would go right along with her young master, but she tried to make some excuse to get away and hide until night, when she would have everything fixed up for her and Sandy. She said she wanted to go to her cabin to get her bonnet. Her missus said it didn't matter about the bonnet, her head-handkerchief was good enough. Then Tenie said she wanted to get her best frock, her missus said no, she didn't need no more frocks, when that one got dirty she could get a clean one where she was going. So Tenie had to get in the buggy and go along with young Master Dunkin to his plantation, which was more than twenty miles away. There wasn't no chance for her seeing Sandy no more, until she came back home. The poor woman felt mighty bad about the way things was going on and she knew Sandy must be a-wondering why she didn't come and turn him back no more.

While Tenie was away nursing young Master Dunkin's wife, Master Marlboro took a notion to build him a new kitchen and being as he had lots of timber on his place, he began to look around for a tree to have the lumber sawed out. I don't know how it came to be

so, but he happened to hit on the very tree Sandy was turned into. Tenie was gone and there wasn't nobody near to watch the tree.

The two men that cut the tree down said they never had such a time with a tree before. Their axes would glance off and didn't appear to make no progress through the wood. And all the creaking, shaking, and wobbling you ever did see, that tree did when he commenced to fall. It was the darndest thing!

When they got the tree all trimmed up, they chained it up to a timber wagon and started for the sawmill. But they had a hard time getting the log there. First they got stuck in the mud when they were going across the swamp and it was two or three hours before they could get out. When they started on again the chain kept coming loose, and they had to keep stopping to hitch the log up again. When they commenced to climb the hill to the sawmill the log broke loose and rolled down the hill and in among the trees and it took about half a day more to get it hauled up to the sawmill.

The next morning after the day the tree was hauled to the sawmill, Tenie came home. When she got back to her cabin, the first thing she did was to run down to the woods and see how Sandy was getting on. When she saw the stump standing there with sap running out of it, and the limbs laying there scattered around, she almost went out of her mind. She ran to her cabin and got her goopher mixture, then followed the tracks of the timber wagon to the sawmill. She knew Sandy couldn't live no more than a minute or so if she turned him back, for he was all chopped up so he had to be dying. But she wanted to turn him back long enough for her to explain that she hadn't gone off on purpose

and left him to be chopped down and sawed up. She didn't want Sandy to die with no hard feelings towards her.

The men at the sawmill had just got the big log on the carriage, and was starting up the saw, when they saw a woman running up the hill all out of breath, crying and going on just like she was plumb distracted. It was Tenie. She came right into the mill and threw herself on the log, right in front of the saw. She was hollering and crying to her Sandy to forgive her, and not think hard of her, for it wasn't no fault of hers. Then Tenie remembered the tree didn't have no ears, and she was getting ready to work her goopher mixture so as to turn Sandy back, when the mill hands caught ahold of her and tied her arms with a rope, fastened her to one of the posts in the sawmill, and then they started the saw up again and cut the log up into boards right before her eyes. But it was mighty hard work, for all the squeaking and moaning and groaning that log did while the saw was going through it.

The saw was one of these there old-timers, up and down saws, and it took longer them days to saw a log then it does now. They greased the saw, but that didn't stop the fuss. It kept right on, until finally they got the log all sawed up.

When the overseer who ran the sawmill came from breakfast the hands told him about the crazy woman that had come running into the sawmill, a-hollering and going on and tried to throw herself before the saw. The overseer sent two or three of the hands to take Tenie back to her master's plantation.

Tenie appeared to be out of her mind for a long time, and her master had to lock her up in the smokehouse until she got over her spells. Master Marlboro

was mighty mad. It would have made your flesh crawl to hear him cuss, because he said the speculator had fooled him by working a crazy woman off on him. While Tenie was locked up in the smokehouse, Master Marlboro took and hauled the lumber from the saw-mill and put up his new kitchen.

When Tenie got quieted down, so she could be allowed to go around the plantation, she up and told her master all about Sandy and the pine tree. When Master Marlboro heard it, he allowed she was the most distracted slave he had ever heard of. He didn't know what to do with Tenie. First he thought he would put her in the poorhouse, but finally, seeing as she didn't do no harm to nobody nor nothing, but just went around moaning and groaning and shaking her head, he decided to let her stay on the plantation and nurse the little black children while their mothers were work-ing in the cotton fields.

The new kitchen Master Marlboro built wasn't much used. It hadn't been put up long before the slaves started to notice queer things about it. They could hear something moaning and groaning about the kitchen in the nighttime and when the wind would blow they could hear something hollering and squeak-ing like it was in great pain and suffering. It got so after a while that it was all Master Marlboro's wife could do to get a woman to stay in the kitchen in the daytime long enough to do the cooking. There wasn't a slave on the plantation that wouldn't rather take forty lashes than to go about that kitchen after dark, that is except Tenie. She didn't appear to mind the spirits. She used to slip around at night and sit on the kitchen steps leaning up against the door, talking to herself with a kind of foolishness that nobody could make out. Master

Marlboro had threatened to send her off the plantation if she said anything to any of the other slaves about the pine tree. But somehow or another the slaves found out all about it and they all knew the kitchen was haunted by Sandy's spirit. It even got so that Master Marlboro's wife herself was scared to go out in the yard after dark.

When it came to that, Master Marlboro tore the kitchen down and used the lumber to build a schoolhouse. The schoolhouse wasn't suppose to be used except in the daytime, but on dark nights folks going along the road would hear queer sounds and see queer things. Poor old Tenie used to go down there at night and wander around the schoolhouse. The slaves all knew that she went to talk with Sandy's spirit.

One winter morning when one of the boys went to school early to start the fire, what should he find but poor old Tenie, lying on the floor, stiff and cold and dead. There didn't appear to be nothing particular the matter with her. She had just grieved herself to death for her Sandy. Master Marlboro didn't shed no tears. He thought Tenie was crazy, and there wasn't no telling what she might do next and he felt there isn't much room in this world for crazy white folks, let alone a crazy nigger.

THE CONJURER'S REVENGE

Primus was a clubfooted slave who used to belong to old Master Jim McGee over on the Lumbington Plank Road. This here Primus was the liveliest hand on the place. He was always a-dancing, drinking, running around, singing, and picking the banjo. Except once in a while, when he would feel he wasn't treated right about something or another. Then he would get so sulky and stubborn that the white folks could hardly do nothing with him.

It was against the rules for any of the hands to go away from the plantation at night; but Primus didn't mind the rules and went when he felt like it. And the white folks pretended like they didn't know it, because Primus was dangerous when he got in them stubborn spells, and they would rather not fool with him.

One night in the spring of the year, Primus slipped off from the plantation and went down on the Wilmington Road to a dance given by some of the free blacks down there. There was a fiddle, and a banjo, and a jug going around on the outside. Primus sung and danced until about two o'clock in the morning.

Then he started for home. He cut through some of the cotton fields along by the edge of Mineral Spring Swamp, so to avoid the patrollers that rode up and down the big road to keep slaves from running around at night. Primus was sauntering along, thinking about the good times he had with the woman. When he was passing a fence he heard something grunt. Then he went over to the fence where he heard the fuss, and there, lying in the corner, on a pile of pine straw, was a fine, fat, young hog.

Primus looked hard at that hog and then started for home. But somehow or another he couldn't get away from that hog. When he took one step forward with one foot, the other foot appeared to take two steps backward, and so he kept naturally getting closer and closer to the hog. It was the darndest thing. The hog just appeared to charm Primus, and the first thing you knew Primus found himself away up the road with the hog on his back.

If Primus had a-known whose hog that was, he would've managed to get past it somehow or another. As it happened, the hog belonged to a conjure man who lived down in the free-black settlement. Of course the conjure man didn't have to work his roots but a little while before he found out who took his hog, and the trouble began.

One morning a day or so later, and before he got a chance to eat the hog up, Primus didn't go to work when the horn blew. When the overseer went to look for him there wasn't no trace of him to be discovered nowhere. When he didn't come back in a day or so everybody on the plantation figured he had ran away. His master advertised him in the papers, and offered a big reward. The slave catchers fetched out their dogs

and tracked him down to the edge of the swamp, and then the scent gave out. That was the last anybody saw of Primus for a long, long time.

Two or three weeks after Primus disappeared, his master went to town one Saturday. Master Jim was standing in front of Sandy Campbell's barroom, up by the old wagon yard, when a poor white man from down on the Wilmington Road came up to him and asked him casually like if he didn't want to buy a mule.

"I don't know," said Master Jim. "It depends on the mule and on the price. Where is the mule?"

"Just around here back of old Tom McAllister's store," said the poor white man.

"I reckon I'll have to look at the mule, and if it suits me, I don't know but what I might buy it."

So the poor white man took Master Jim around back of the store, and there stood a mighty fine mule. When the mule saw Master Jim he gave a whinny, just like he knew him before. Master Jim looked at the mule, and it appeared to be sound and strong. There was something familiar about the mule's face, especially his eyes. But Master Jim hadn't lost a mule, and didn't have no remembrance of having seen the animal before. He asked the poor white man where he got the mule, and he told him his brother raised him down on Rockfish Creek. Master Jim was a little suspicious of seeing a poor white man with such a fine creature, but he finally agreed to give him fifty dollars for the mule, about half of what a good mule was worth them days.

He tied the mule behind the buggy and got him home. The next day he put him to plowing cotton. The mule did mighty well for three or four days. Then the slaves commenced to notice some queer things about him. There was a meadow on the plantation

where they used to put the horses and mules to pasture. It was fenced off from the cotton field on one side, but on the other side of the pasture was a tobacco patch that wasn't fenced off, because everybody knows animals don't like tobacco. The slaves noticed the first thing the new mule did, when he was turned to the pasture, was to head straight for the tobacco plants. After that they had to put a halter on him, and tie him to a stake, or else there wouldn't have been a leaf of tobacco left in the patch.

Another day one of the hands hitched up the mule and drove over to Master Dugal's vineyard. Master Dugal had killed a yearling and the neighboring white folks all sent over for some fresh beef. Master Jim had sent this hand over for some too. There was a winepress in the yard where the mule was left standing, and in front of the press there was a tub of grape juice, just pressed out, and a little to one side a barrel about half full of wine that had been standing two or three days and had begun to get sort of sharp to the taste. There was a couple of boards on top of this barrel, with a rock laid on them to hold them down. As I was saying, this hand left the mule standing in the yard and went into the smokehouse to get the beef. By and by, when he came out, he saw the mule a-staggering about the yard, and before the hand could get there and find out what was the matter, the mule fell right over on his side and lay there just like he was dead.

All the slaves about the house ran out there to see what was the matter. Some said the mule had cholera. Some said one thing or another, until by and by one of the slaves saw the top was off the barrel, and ran and looked in.

"That mule has been drinking the wine," he

screamed. And sure enough, the mule had passed right by the tub of fresh grape juice and pushed the cover off the barrel and drank two or three gallons of the wine that had been standing long enough to begin to get sharp.

The slaves all made a great admiration about the mule getting drunk. They never had seen nothing like it in their born days. They poured water over the mule, and tried to sober him up. But it wasn't no use, and the hand had to take the beef home on his back, and leave the mule there, until he slept off his spree.

I don't remember if I told you or not, but when Primus disappeared from the plantation, he left a wife behind him, a mighty good-looking yellow girl named Sally. When Primus had been gone a month or so, Sally commenced to get lonesome and took up with another young man named Dan who belonged to the same plantation. One day this here Dan took the new mule out in the cotton field to do some plowing. And when they were going along the rows, who should he meet but Sally. Dan looked around and he didn't see the overseer nowhere, so he stopped a minute to talk to Sally.

They were looking at one another, and they didn't pay no attention to the mule, who had turned his head around and was looking at Sally as hard as he could, and stretching his neck and raising his ears, and whinnying kind of soft to himself.

"Yes, honey," said Dan, "and you're going to feel first-rate as long as you stick to me. I'm a better man than that low-down runaway Primus that you've been wasting your time with."

Dan had let go of the plow handle and had put his arm around Sally and was just going to kiss her, when

something caught him by the back of the neck and flung him away over in the cotton patch. When he picked himself up, Sally had gone tearing down through the rows, and the mule was standing there looking as calm and peaceful as a Sunday morning.

First Dan had allowed it was the overseer who had caught him wasting his time. But there wasn't no overseer in sight, so he concluded it must have been the mule. So he pitched into the mule and whipped him as hard as he could.

The mule took it all and appeared to be as humble as a mule could be; but when they were making the turn at the end of a row, one of the plow lines got under the mule's hind legs. Dan reached to get the line out, sort of careless like, when the mule hauled off and kicked him clean over the fence in a brier patch on the other side.

Dan was mighty sore from his wounds and scratches, and was laid up for two or three days. One night the new mule got out of the pasture and went down to the quarters. Dan was lying there on his pallet, when he heard something banging away at the side of his cabin. He raised up on one shoulder and looked around, when what should he see but the new mule's head sticking in the window, with his lips drawn back over his teeth, grinning and snapping at Dan just like he wanted to eat him up. Then the mule went around to the door, and kicked away like he wanted to break it down, until somebody came along and drove him back to the pasture. When Sally came in a little later from the big house, where she had been waiting on the white folks, she found poor Dan nigh about dead, he was so scared. She allowed Dan had had a nightmare; but she looked at the door, and saw the marks of the mule's hoofs, so

21

there couldn't have been no mistake about what had happened.

Of course the slaves told their master about the mule's goings-on. First he didn't pay no attention to it, but after a while he told them if they didn't stop their foolishness, he was going to tie them up. So after that they didn't say nothing more to the master, but they kept on noticing the mule's queer ways.

Along about the middle of the summer, there was a camp meeting down on Wilmington Road. And just about every poor white and free black got religion. Among them was the conjure man, who owned the young hog that charmed Primus.

The conjure man decided to get religion. But he kneeled so long at the mourners' bench that he caught a cold and got real sick. He kept getting worse and worse, and by and by the rheumatism took hold of him and drew him all up. Until one day he sent word up to Master Jim McGee's plantation and asked Pete, the slave that took care of the mules, to come down there that night and fetch that mule that his master had bought from the poor white man during the summer.

Pete didn't know what the conjure man was driving at, but he didn't dare stay away. So that night after dinner he put a bridle on the mule and rode him down to the conjure man's cabin. When he got to the door, he hitched the mule and then knocked on the door. He felt mighty dubious about going in, but he knew he'd better.

"Pull the string," said a weak voice, and Pete lifted the latch and went in. The conjure man was lying on the bed, looking pale and weak, like he didn't have much longer to live. "Have you fetched the mule?"

Pete said yes, and the conjure man went on. "Brother Pete, I've been a mighty sinning man. I've done a powerful lot of wickedness during my days. But the good Lord has washed my sins away and I feel now that I'm bound for the kingdom. I feel, too, that I ain't going to get up from this bed no more in this world, and I want to undo some of the harm I've done. And that's the reason, Brother Pete, that I've sent for you, to fetch that mule down here. You remember that young hog I was up to your plantation inquiring about last June?"

"Yes," said Brother Pete, "I remember your asking about a young hog you had lost."

"I don't know if you found out or not, but I found out that Primus had taken the hog, and I was determined to get even with him. So one night I caught him down by the swamp, and I threw a goopher mixture on him, and turned him to a mule, and got a poor white man to sell the mule and we divided the money. But I don't want to die until I turn Brother Primus back again."

Then the conjure man asked Pete to take down one or two of the jars with some kind of mixture in them and set them on a stool by the bed, and then he asked him to fetch the mule.

When the mule came in the door, he gave a snort and started for the bed, just like he was going to jump on it.

"Hold on there, Brother Primus," hollered the conjure man. "I'm mighty weak, and if you commence on me, you won't never have no chance of getting turned back."

The mule saw the sense of that, and stood still. Then the conjure man kept on working his roots, and

Pete and Primus could see he was getting weaker and weaker all the time.

"Brother Pete," he said, "give me a drink of them bitters out of that green bottle on the shelf a-yonder. I'm going fast, and it'll give me strength to finish this work."

Pete looked up on the mantelpiece and he saw a bottle in the corner. It was so dark in the cabin he couldn't tell whether it was a green bottle or not. But he held the bottle to the conjure man's mouth, and he took a big mouthful. He had no more than swallowed it before he commenced to holler.

"You gave me the wrong bottle, it's got poison in it, and I'm done for it this time. Hold me up, until I get through turning Primus back."

So Pete held him up, and he kept on working the roots, until he got the goopher all taken off Primus except one foot. He hadn't got this foot more than half turned back before his strength gave out entirely and he dropped the roots and fell back on the bed.

"I can't do no more for you, Brother Primus," he said, "but I hope you'll forgive me for what harm I've done you. I know the good Lord done forgave me, and I hope to meet you again in glory. I see the good angels waiting for me up yonder, with a long white robe and a starry crown, and I'm on my way to join them." And so the conjure man died, and Pete and Primus went back to the plantation.

The slaves all made a great commotion when Primus came back. Master Jim let on like he didn't believe the tale. He said Primus had run away and stayed until he got tired of the swamps and then come back to get fed. He tried to account for the shape of Primus's foot by saying Primus got his foot smashed,

or snakebit, or something while he was away, and then stayed out in the woods where he couldn't get it fixed up. But the slaves all noticed the master didn't have Primus whipped, nor carry on too much about the mule being gone. So they figured the master must have had his suspicions about the conjure man.

THE GRAY WOLF'S HAINT

Long before the war, Old Master Dugal used to own a slave named Dan. Dan was big and strong, hearty, peaceable, and good-natured most of the time. But dangerous if aggravated. He always did his work and never had any trouble with the white folks. But woe be to the slave that fooled with Dan, for he was sure to get a good beating. Soon as everybody found Dan out, didn't many of them attempt to disturb him. The ones that did would soon wish they hadn't, if they had lived long enough to do any wishing.

Now, there was a conjure man who lived on the other side of the Lumbington Road. He had been the only conjure doctor in the neighborhood for many years, until Aunt Peggy set up business down by the Wilmington Road. This conjure man had a son that lived with him. It was this son that got mixed up with Dan, and it was all about a woman.

There was a woman on the plantation named Mahaly. She was a mighty likely woman, tall and supple, with big eyes, a small foot, and a lively tongue. When Dan took to going with her, everyone said they

were well matched. None of the other men on the plantation went near her, for they were all afraid of Dan.

Now it so happened that this here conjure man's son was going along the road one day, and who should come past but Mahaly. The minute this man set eyes on Mahaly, he wanted to talk to her. But she didn't pay any attention to him because she was thinking about Dan, and she didn't like the way this man was looking anyway. So when she got to where she was going this here man wasn't no further along than he was when he started.

Of course, Dan got mad when he heard about this man pestering Mahaly, and the next night when he saw him coming along the road, he up and asked him what he meant by hanging around his woman. The man didn't respond to suit Dan, and one word led to another until by and by this conjure man's son pulled out a knife and started to stick it in Dan. But before he could get it drawn good, Dan hauled off and hit him in the head so hard that he never got up. Dan figured he would come to after a while and go along about his business, so he went off and left him lying there on the ground.

The next morning the man was found dead. There was a great commotion about it, but Dan didn't say nothing. Since no one had seen the fight, there wasn't a way to tell who had done the killing. And being that the conjurer's son was a free black, no whites were especially interested, so nothing was done about it. The conjure man came and took his son and carried him away and buried him.

Now Dan hadn't meant to kill this man, and while he knew the man hadn't got no more than he deserved,

Dan started to worry more or less. For he knew this man's daddy would work his roots and probably find out who had killed his son. Dan kept on thinking about this until he got so he hardly ate or drank, fearing that the conjure man had poisoned his food or water. Finally he decided to go down by the Wilmington Road and see Aunt Peggy. Maybe she could do something to protect him from this conjure man. So he took a basket of potatoes and went down to her cabin one night.

After Aunt Peggy had heard his tale, she said, "That conjure man is more than twice as old as I am, and he can make a mighty powerful goopher. What you need is a life-charm. It's the only thing that will do you any good. I'll make you one tomorrow. You leave me a couple of hairs from your head, and fetch me a good roasting pig tomorrow night. And when you come, I'll have the charm all ready for you."

Dan went down to Aunt Peggy the next night. He carried a tender young pig. Aunt Peggy gave him the charm. She had taken the hair Dan had left with her, a piece of red flannel, some roots, some herbs, and had put them in a little bag made out of coonskin.

"You take this charm," she told him, "and put it in a bottle or a tin box, and bury it deep under the root of a live-oak tree. As long as it stays there safe and sound, there ain't no poison that can poison you. There ain't no rattlesnake that can bite you. There ain't no scorpion that can sting you. This here conjure man might do one thing or another to you, but he can't kill you. You need not be scared; go along about your business and don't bother your mind."

Dan went down by the river and way up the bank. He buried the charm deep under the root of a live-oak

tree and covered it up and stomped the dirt down and scattered leaves over the spot, and then went home with his mind at ease.

Sure enough, this here conjure man worked his roots, just as Dan had expected. He soon learned who killed his son. And of course he made up his mind to get even with Dan. He sent a rattlesnake but the snake found Dan's heels so hard he couldn't get his fangs in. Then he sent a jaybird to put poison in Dan's food, but the poison didn't work.

Then the conjure man figured he would double Dan all up with rheumatism, so he couldn't get his hand to his mouth to eat, and would have to starve to death. But Dan went to Aunt Peggy, and she gave him an ointment for rheumatism. Next, the conjure man decided to burn Dan up with the fever, but Aunt Peggy told him how to make some herb tea for that. Nothing this man tried would kill Dan, so finally the conjure man knew Dan must have a life-charm.

Now the jaybird that conjure man had was mighty smart. In fact the slaves said the bird was the old devil himself, just sitting around waiting to carry this old man away when he reached the end of his rope. The conjure man sent his jaybird to watch Dan and find out where he kept his charm. The jaybird hung around Dan for a week or so, and one day he saw Dan go down by the river and look at a live-oak tree. The jaybird went back to his master and told him he suspected Dan kept his life-charm under a tree.

The conjure man laughed and laughed. Then he put on his biggest pot, filled it with his strangest root, and boiled and boiled it, until by and by wind blew and blew until it blew down to the live-oak tree. Then he stirred some more roots in the pot and it rained

and rained until the water ran down the riverbank and washed Dan's life-charm into the river. The bottle went bobbing down the river with the current just as unconcerned as if it wasn't taking poor Dan's chances along with it. Then the conjure man laughed some more and promised himself he was going to fix Dan now, sure enough. He wasn't going to kill him just yet—he wanted to do something to him that was worse than killing him.

The conjure man started going up to Dan's cabin every night and taking Dan out in his sleep and riding him around the roads, the fields, and over the rough grounds. In the morning Dan would be as tired as he had been before going to sleep. This kind of thing kept up for over a week, and Dan had just about made up his mind to go see Aunt Peggy again when who should he come across, going along the road one day, but the conjure man. Dan felt kind of scared at first, but he remembered his life-charm, which he hadn't been to see for a week or more. But he figured it was safe and sound under the live-oak tree. So he held his head up and walked along, just like he didn't care nothing about this conjure man.

When he got close to the conjure man, the conjure man said:

"Howdy, Brother Dan. I hope you're well?"

When Dan saw the conjure man was in a good humor, and didn't appear to bear no malice, Dan allowed maybe the conjure man hadn't found out who had killed his son. So Dan played along like he didn't know either, and asked the conjure man how *he* was feeling.

"I'm feeling as well as an old man can feel who has lost his only son. But my son was a bad boy, and I guess

I couldn't expect nothing else. I tried to learn him the error of his way, and make him go to church and prayer meeting, but it was no use. I don't know who killed him, and I don't want to know, for I would be sure to find out that my son started it first. If I had had a son like you, Brother Dan, I would have been a proud man. But you ain't looking so well as you should. There's something the matter with you, and what's more, I expect you don't know what it is."

Now this here kind of talk naturally threw Dan off his guard. The first thing he knew he was talking to the conjure man just like he was one of his best friends. He told him all about not feeling well in the morning, and asked him if he could tell what was the matter with him.

"Yes," said the conjure man. "There is a witch that's been riding you right along. I can see the marks of the bridle on your mouth. And I'll bet your back is raw where she's been beating you."

"Yes," responded Dan, "so it is." He hadn't noticed it before, but now he felt just like his hide had been taken off of him.

"And your thighs are just as raw where the spurs have been driving in you. You can't see the raw spots, but you can feel them."

"Oh yes," said Dan, "they do hurt mighty bad."

"And what's more," said the conjure man, coming up close to Dan and whispering in his ear, "I know who it is that's riding you."

"Who is it?" asked Dan. "Tell me who it is."

"It's an old woman down by Rockfish Creek. She had a pet rabbit, and you caught him one day, and she's been squaring up with you ever since. But you better

stop her, or else you'll be ridden to death in a month or so."

"No," said Dan. "She can't kill me for sure."

"I don't know how that is," said the conjure man. "But she can make your life mighty miserable. If I was in your place, I'd stop her right off."

"But how am I going to stop her? I don't know nothing about stopping witches."

"Look here, Dan. You are a good man. I like you mighty well. In fact, I feel like one of these days I might buy you from your master and adopt you for my own son. I like you so well that I'm going to help you get rid of this here witch for good. Because as long as she lives, you're going to have trouble, and more trouble."

And Dan said, "You're the best friend I got. I'll remember your kindness to my dying day. Tell me how I can get rid of this here old witch that's been riding me so hard."

"In the first place, this old witch never comes in her own shape," answered the conjure man. "Every night, at ten, she turns herself into a black cat and runs down to your cabin and bridles you and mounts you, and drives you through the chimney and rides you over the roughest places she can find. All you got to do is to wait for her in the bushes beside your cabin and hit her in the head with a rock when she goes past."

"But how can I see her in the dark? And supposing I hit at her and miss? Supposing I just wound her, and she gets away, what's she going to do to me next?"

"I've studied about all them things, and it appears that the best plan for you to follow is to let me turn you

to some creature that can see in the dark. One that can run just as fast as a cat. One that can bite to kill. Then you won't have no trouble after the job is done. I don't know whether you like that or not, but that is the surest way."

"I'll be anything for an hour or so if I can kill that old witch. You can do just what you have a mind to."

"All right, then, you come down to my cabin at half past nine o'clock tonight, and I'll fix you up."

Now the conjure man kept going down the road, until he met Mahaly coming home from her work.

"Howdy do," he said. "Is your name Sister Mahaly who belongs to Master Dugal?"

"Yes," said Mahaly, "that's my name, and I belong to Master Dugal."

"Well, your husband, Dan, was down by my cabin this evening, and he got bit by a spider or something, and his foot is swollen up, so he can't walk. He asked me to find you and fetch you down there to help him home."

Of course Mahaly wanted to see what had happened to Dan, so she started down the road with the conjure man. As soon as he got her into his cabin, he shut the door and sprinkled some goopher mixture on her. And turned her into a black cat. Then he took her and put her in a barrel, and put a board on the barrel and a rock on the board and left her there until he got good and ready to use her.

Along about half past nine, Dan came down to the conjure man's cabin. It was a warm night and the door was standing open. The conjure man invited Dan to come in and pass the time of day with him. As soon as Dan started talking, he heard a cat meowing, and scratching, and going on at a terrible rate.

34

"What's all that noise about?" asked Dan.

"Oh, that ain't nothing but my old gray tomcat. I have to shut him up sometimes to keep him in at nights." Then the conjure man went on. "Now, let me tell you just what you got to do when you catch this witch. You must take her right by the throat and bite her right through the neck. Be sure your teeth go through at the first bite, and then you won't be bothered no more by that witch. When you get done, come back here and I'll turn you back to yourself again, so you can go home and get a good night's rest."

The conjure man gave Dan something nice and sweet to drink. In about a minute Dan found himself turned to a gray wolf. Soon as he felt all four of his new feet on the floor, he started off fast as he could to his own cabin.

When Dan was gone, the conjure man took the rock off the board and the board off the barrel and out leaped Mahaly and started for home, just like a cat or a woman or anybody else would if they were in trouble. It wasn't many minutes before she was going up the path to her own door.

Meanwhile, when Dan had reached the cabin, he hid himself in a bunch of jimsonweeds in the yard. He hadn't waited long before he saw a black cat run up the path towards the door. Just as soon as she got close to him, he leaped out and caught her by the throat and got a grip on her, just like the conjure man had told him to do. But no sooner had the blood commenced to flow than the black cat turned back to Mahaly, and Dan saw that he had killed his own wife.

While her breath was giving out, she called, "Oh Dan, Dan, come and help me. Save me from this wolf that's killing me."

When poor Dan started towards her, trying to help, Mahaly screamed louder, not knowing that the wolf was Dan. Dan had to hide in the weeds, gritting his teeth and holding himself until she passed out of her misery, calling for Dan to the last, and wondering why he didn't come and help her. Dan would have rather been killed a dozen times than done what he had done to Mahaly.

Dan was mighty near distracted, but when Mahaly was dead and he got his mind straightened out a little, it didn't take him more than a minute or so to see through the conjure man's lies. And how the conjure man had fooled him and made him kill Mahaly, in order to get even with him for killing his son. Dan kept getting madder and madder, and Mahaly hadn't much drawn her last breath before he started back to the conjure man's cabin as fast as he could.

When he got there, the door was open. A fire was burning and the old conjure man was sitting there nodding in the corner. Dan leaped in the door and jumped for this man's throat, and got the same grip on him as the conjure man had said. It was hard work this time, for the old man's neck was mighty tough and stringy, but Dan held on long enough to be sure the job was done right. And even then he didn't hold on long enough. When he turned the conjure man loose, and he fell on the floor, the conjure man rolled his eyes at Dan, and said:

"I'm even with you, Brother Dan, and you are even with me. You killed my son, and I killed your woman. I don't want no more than what is fair about this thing. If you reach up with your paw and take down that bottle and take a sip of the mixture it will turn you

back to a man again and I can die more satisfied than if I left you like this."

Dan never for a minute thought that the man would lie with his last breath, and of course he could see the sense in getting turned back to a man before the conjure man died. So he climbed up on a chair and got the bottle and took a sip. And as soon as he had done that, the conjure man laughed his last breath, and gasped out with his last gasp:

"Uh huh! I reckon I square with you now for killing me, too. That goopher on you is done fixed and set now for good, and all the conjuring in the world won't never take it off.

"WOLF YOU ARE AND WOLF YOU STAY ALL THE REST OF YOUR BORN DAYS!"

Of course Brother Dan couldn't do nothing. He knew it wasn't no use, but he climbed up on the chimney where the shelf was, and got down the bottles of other conjuring fixings and tried them all on himself. Then he ran down to old Aunt Peggy's, but she didn't know the wolf language and couldn't have taken off the goopher anyhow, even if she had understood what Dan was saying. So poor Dan had to remain a wolf all the rest of his born days.

They found Mahaly down by her own cabin the next morning. Everybody was surprised by the way she had been killed. They were convinced it was by a wolf. But the white folks said no, that there hadn't been no wolf around here for ten years or more. They didn't know what to make of it. When they couldn't find Dan nowhere, they figured he had a fight with Mahaly and killed her and had run away. They didn't know what

to make of that, because Dan and Mahaly was the most loving couple on the plantation. They put the dogs on Dan's scent, and tracked him down to the conjure man's cabin, and found the old man dead, and they didn't know what to make of that. Then Dan's scent gave out, and they didn't know what to make of that.

Mahaly was buried down in the low-lying ground. Poor Dan didn't have nowhere else to go, so he just stayed around Mahaly's grave, when he wasn't out in the woods getting something to eat. Sometimes at night some of the slaves used to hear him howling and howling down there. Then some other slaves said they saw Mahaly's haint talking with this gray wolf. After Dan died and dried up in the woods, his haint and Mahaly's stayed there in that low-lying piece of ground where she was buried. Anyone who goes down there has some bad luck or something, because haints don't like to be disturbed on their own stomping ground.

MASTER JAMES' NIGHTMARE

Master James McLean had a big plantation and alot of slaves. Master James was a hard man, and mighty strict with his hands. Ever since he grew up he never appeared to have no feeling for nobody. When his daddy, Old Master John McLean, died, the plantation and all the slaves fell to young Master James. He had been bad before, but it wasn't long afterwards until he got so there was no use in living at all if you had to live around Master James. His slaves worked from dawn to way after dark. Other folks' slaves didn't have to work except from sun to sun. They weren't allowed to sing, dance, nor play the banjo when Master James was around the place. Master James said he wouldn't have no such goings-on, said he bought his hands to work and not to play, and when night come they must sleep and rest, so they would be ready to get up soon in the morning and go to their work fresh and strong.

And Master James didn't allow no courting around his plantation. He said he wanted his slaves to put their minds on their work, and not be wasting their time with such foolishness. He wouldn't let his hands get

married, said he wasn't raising slaves, but was raising cotton. Whenever any of the slaves commenced to get sweet on one another, he would sell one or the other of them or send one way down in Robinson County to his other plantation, where they couldn't see one another.

If any of the slaves ever complained, they got forty; so of course many didn't complain. But they didn't like it just the same. Master James didn't make no allowances for natural-born laziness, nor sickness, nor trouble in the mind, not nothing. He was just going to get so much work out of every hand, or know the reason why.

There was one time the slaves allowed, for a spell at least, that Master James might get better. He took a liking to Master Marlboro's oldest daughter, Miss Libbie, and he used to go over there every day and every evening. Folks said they were going to get married. But it appeared that Miss Libbie heard about the goings-on on Master James' plantation, and she just allowed she couldn't trust herself with no such man. That he might get so used to abusing his slaves that he would commence to abuse his wife after he got used to having her around the house. So she declared she was going to have nothing more to do with young Master James.

The slaves were all mighty sorry when the match was all busted up, for now Master James got worst than he was before he started sweethearting. The time he used to spend courting Miss Libbie he put in finding fault with the slaves, and all his bad feelings, cause Miss Libbie threw him over, he appeared to try to work out on his poor slaves.

Now while Master James was courting Miss Libbie,

two of the hands on the plantation had got to setting a heap of store by one another. One of them was named Solomon, and the other was a woman that worked in the field along with him. I forget that woman's name, but it don't amount to much in the tale, nohow. Now whether because Master James was so taken up with his own courting that he didn't pay no attention for a while to what was going on between Solomon and his girl, or whether his own courting made him kind of easy on the courting in the quarters, there's no way of knowing. But there is one thing for sure, that when Miss Libbie threw him over he found out about Solomon and the girl mighty quick. He gave him forty, and sent the girl down to the Robinson County plantation, and told all the other slaves if he caught them at any more such foolishness, he was going to skin them alive and tan their hides before their very eyes. So you can imagine there wasn't much love going on in the quarters for a long time.

Master James used to go down to the other plantation sometimes for a week or more. He had the overseer to look after his work while he was gone. Master James' overseer was a poor white man named Nick Johnson. The slaves called him Master Johnson to his face, but behind his back they used to call him Old Nick, and the name suited him to a T. He was worst than Master James ever dared to be. Of course the slaves didn't like the way Master James used them, but he was the Master, and had a right to do as he pleased. But this here Old Nick wasn't nothing but a poor white trash, and the slaves despised him as much as they hated him. He didn't own nobody, and wasn't no better than a slave, for in those days any respectable person would rather be a black slave than a poor white man.

Now, after Solomon's girl had been sent away, he kept feeling more and more bad about it, until he finally allowed he was going to see if there couldn't be something done to get her back, and to make Master James treat the slaves better. So he took a peck of cotton out of the barn one night, and went over to see old Aunt Peggy, the free black conjuring woman down by the Wilmington Road.

Aunt Peggy listened to his tale and asked him some questions, and told him she would work her roots, and see what they would say about it, and tomorrow night he should come back again and fetch another peck of cotton, and then she would have something to tell him.

So Solomon went back the next night, and sure enough, Aunt Peggy told him what to do. She gave him some stuff that looked like it had been made by pounding up some roots and herbs with a pestle and mortar.

"This here stuff," she said, "is a mighty powerful goopher. You take this home, and give it to the cook, if you can trust her. Tell her to put it in your master's soup the first cloudy day he has okra soup for dinner. Mind you follow the directions."

"It ain't going to poison him, is it?" asked Solomon, getting kind of scared. Solomon was a good man, and didn't want to do nobody no real harm.

"Oh, no," said old Aunt Peggy, "it's going to do him good, but he'll have a mighty bad dream first. A month from now you come down here and let me know how the goopher is working. I ain't done much of this kind of conjuring of late, and I have to kind of keep track of it to see that I don't accomplish no more than I allowed for it to do. And I have to be kind of careful about conjuring white folks. So be sure and let me

46

know, whatever you do, just what is going on around the plantation."

So Solomon said all right, and took the goopher mixture up to the big house and gave it to the cook. He told her to put it in Master James' soup the first cloudy day she made okra soup for dinner. It happened that the very next day was a cloudy day, and so the cook made okra soup for Master James' dinner. She put the powder Solomon gave her into the soup, and made the soup real good, so Master James would eat a whole lot of it, and he appeared to enjoy it.

The next morning, Master James told the overseer he was going away on some business, and then he was going to his other plantation down in Robinson County, and he didn't expect he would be back for a month or so.

But says he, "I want you to run this here plantation for all it's worth. These here slaves are getting mighty trifling lazy and careless. I want that to stop. And while I'm gone away, I want to cut expenses way down and a heap more work done. In fact, I want this here plantation to make a record that'll show what kind of overseer you are."

Old Nick didn't say nothing except, "Yes, sir!" But the way he kind of grinned to himself and showed his big yellow teeth, and snapped the rawhide he carried around with him made cold chills run up and down the backbone of the slaves that heard Master James a-talking. And that night there was moaning and groaning down in the quarters, for the slaves all knew what was coming.

So, sure enough, Master James went away the next morning, and the trouble began. Master Johnson

started off the very first day to see what he could have to show Master James when he came back. He made the tasks bigger and the rations smaller. When the slaves had worked all day, he would find something for them to do around the barn or somewhere after dark. He kept them busy until a hour or so before they went to sleep.

About three or four days after Master James went away, young Master Dunkin McSwayne rode up to the big house with a slave sitting behind him in the buggy, tied to the seat, and asked if Master James was home. Master Johnson was at the house, and he said, "No."

"Well," said Master Dunkin, "I fetched this slave over to Mister McLean to pay a bet I made with him last week when we were playing cards together. I bet him a slave man, and here's one I reckon will fill the bill. He was taken up the other day as a stray, and he couldn't give any account of himself, so he was sold at an auction. I bought him. He's kind of brash, but I know your powers, Mister Johnson, and I reckon if anybody can make him toe the mark you are the man."

Master Johnson grinned one of them grins that showed all of his snaggled teeth, and made the slaves allow he looked like the old devil himself, and said to Master Dunkin:

"I reckon you can trust me, Mister Dunkin, to tame any slave ever born. The slave doesn't live that I can't take down in about four days."

Well, Old Nick had his hands full with that new slave. And while the rest of the slaves were sorry for that poor man, they allowed he kept Master Johnson so busy that they got along better than they would have done if the new slave had never come.

The first thing that happened, Master Johnson said

to this here new man: "What's your name, Sambo?"

"My name ain't Sambo," responded the new slave.

"Didn't I ask you what your name was?" said Master Johnson. "You want to be particular how you talk to me. Now what is your name and where did you come from?"

"I don't know my name," said the slave. "And I don't remember where I came from. My head is all kind of mixed up."

"Yes, I reckon I'll have to give you something to clear your head. At the same time, it'll learn you some manners, and after this maybe you'll say 'Sir' when you speak to me."

Well, Master Johnson hauled off and hit the new slave with his rawhide. The new man looked at Master Johnson for a minute as if he didn't know what to make of this here kind of learning. But when the overseer raised his whip to hit him again, the new slave just hauled off and made for Master Johnson and if some of the other slaves hadn't stopped him, it appeared as if he might have made it warm for Old Nick there for a while. But the overseer made the other slaves tie the new one up. Then he gave him forty with a dozen or so thrown in for good measure.

Master Johnson locked the new slave up in the barn, and didn't give him anything to eat for a day or so, until he got him kind of quieted down, then he turned him loose and put him to work. But the slave allowed he wasn't used to working and wouldn't work. Master Johnson gave him another forty for laziness and impudence, and let him fast for another day or so. Then he put him to work again. He went to work but didn't appear to know how to handle a hoe. It took just about half the overseer's time looking after him.

That poor slave got more lashings, cursings, and beatings than any four other slaves.

The new slave didn't mix with nor talk much to the rest of the slaves. He couldn't appear to get it through his mind that he was a slave and had to work and mind the white folks, in spite of the fact that Old Nick gave him a lesson every day. Finally Master Johnson allowed that he couldn't do nothing with him, that if he was his slave, he would break his spirit or his neck. One or the other. But of course he was only sent over on trial, and as he didn't give satisfaction, he could send him back before he killed him. So he tied him up and sent him back to Master Dunkin.

Now, Master Dunkin McSwayne was one of these here easygoing gentlemen that didn't like to have no trouble with slaves nor nobody else, and he knew if Old Nick couldn't get along with this slave, nobody could. So he took the slave to town that same day and sold him to a trader who was getting up a gang to ship off on a steamboat for New Orleans.

The next day after the new man had been sent away, Solomon was working in the cotton field. When he got to the fence next to the woods, at the end of the row, who should he see on the other side but old Aunt Peggy. She beckoned to him.

"Why ain't you done come and reported to me like I told you?"

"Why Aunt Peggy," said Solomon, "there ain't nothing to report. Master James went away the day after we gave him the goopher mixture, and we ain't seen hide nor hair of him since. So of course we don't know nothing about what effect it had on him."

"I don't care nothing about your Master James now. What's been going on among the slaves? Have

you been getting along any better on the plantation?"

"No, Aunt Peggy, it's been getting worse. Master Johnson is stricter than he ever was before, and the poor slaves don't hardly get time to draw their breath, and they allow they might as well be dead as alive."

"Uh huh!" said Aunt Peggy, "I told you that was a mighty powerful goopher, and its work don't appear all at once."

"As long as we had that new slave here, he kept Master Johnson busy most of the time, but now he's gone away. I suppose the rest of us will catch it worst than ever."

"What went on with this new slave?" asked Aunt Peggy real quick, batting her eyes and straightening up.

"Old Nick done sent him back to Master Dunkin, who had fetched him here to pay a gambling debt to Master James," he told her. "And I hear Master Dunkin has sold him to a slave trader who's going to ship him off with a gang tomorrow."

Old Aunt Peggy appeared to get really stirred up when he told her that.

"Why didn't you come and tell me about this new slave being sold away? Didn't you promise me, if I'd give you that goopher, you would come and report to me about all that was going on, on the plantation?" she said, shaking her stick at him. "Of course I could've found out for myself, but I depended on you telling me, and now by not doing it, I'm afraid you're going to spoil my conjuring. You come down to my house tonight and do what I tell you, or I'll put a spell on you that will make your hair fall out so you'll be bald, and your eyes drop out so you can't see, and your teeth fall out so you can't eat, and your ears grow up so you

can't hear. When you're fooling with a conjure woman like me, you got to mind your P's and Q's, or there will be trouble sure enough."

So of course Solomon went down to Aunt Peggy's that night. She gave him a roasted sweet potato.

"You take this here sweet potato. I done goophered it especially for that new slave, so you better not eat it yourself or you'll wish you hadn't. Slip off to town and find that new slave, and give him this here sweet potato. He must eat it before morning, sure enough, if he doesn't want to be sold away to New Orleans."

"But suppose the patrollers catch me, Aunt Peggy, what am I going to do?"

"Ain't nobody going to catch you, but if you don't find that slave, I'm going to get you, and you'll find me worse than any patrollers. Just hold on a minute, and I'll sprinkle you with some of this mixture out of this here bottle, so nobody can see you. You can rub your feet with some of this grease out of this jar, so you can run fast, and rub some of it on your eyes so you can see in the dark."

Solomon took the sweet potato and started up the road as fast as he could go, and before long he reached town. He went right along by the patrollers, and they didn't appear to notice him. By and by he found where the strange slave was kept, and he walked right past the guard at the door and found him.

The strange slave was lying in a corner, asleep, and Solomon just slipped up to him and held the sweet potato next to his nose. And he just naturally reached up with his hand and took the potato and ate it in his sleep, without knowing it. When Solomon saw he had eaten the potato, he went back and told Aunt Peggy, and then went home to his cabin to sleep.

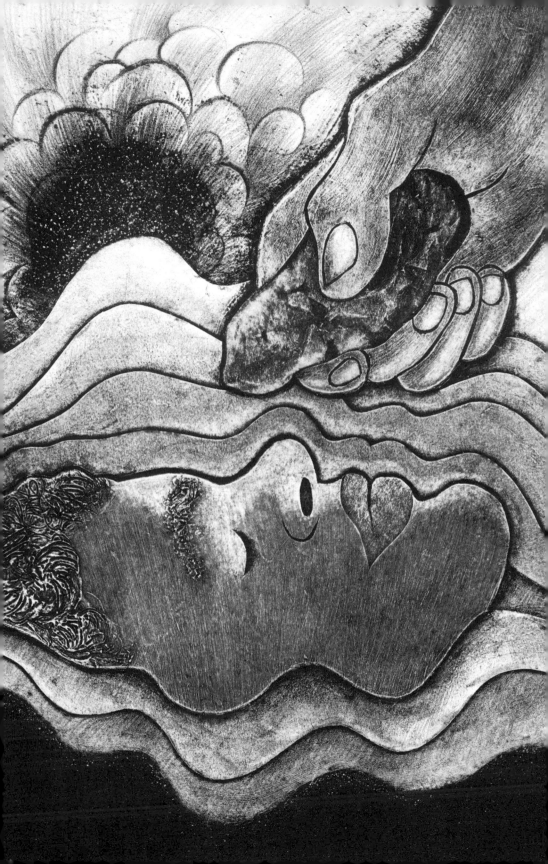

The next day was Sunday, so the slaves had a little time for themselves. Solomon was kind of disturbed in his mind, thinking about his sweetheart that had gone away, but he also wondered what Aunt Peggy had to do with that new slave. He had sauntered up in the woods so to be by himself a little and at the same time to look after a rabbit trap he had set down on the edge of the swamp, when who should he see standing under a tree but a white man.

Solomon didn't know the white man at first, until the white man spoke up to him. "Is that you, Solomon?"

Then Solomon recognized the voice. "For the Lord's sake, Master James, is that you?"

"Yes, Solomon, this is me, or what's left of me."

It wasn't surprising that Solomon hadn't recognized Master James at first. He was dressed like a poor white man. He was barefooted and looked mighty pale and peaked, as if he had just come through a spell of sickness.

"You're looking kind of poorly, Master James," said Solomon. "Have you been sick, sir?"

"No, Solomon," he said, shaking his head, and speaking sort of slow and sad. "I ain't been sick, but I've had a mighty bad dream, fact is, a regular natural nightmare. But tell me how things been going on at the plantation since I've been gone, Solomon."

So Solomon up and told him about the crops and about the horses and the mules, and about the cows and the hogs. When he commenced to tell about the new slave, Master James picked up his ears and listened, and every now and then he said, "Uh huh! Uh huh!" By and by when he had asked Solomon some more questions, he said:

"Now, Solomon, I don't want you to say a word to nobody about meeting me here, but I want you to slip up to the house and fetch me some clothes and some shoes. I forgot to tell you a man robbed me back yonder on the road and swapped clothes with me without asking me. But you don't need to say nothing about that, neither. You go on and fetch me some clothes here, so nobody won't see you, and keep your mouth shut, and I'll give you a dollar."

Solomon was so astonished he like to fell over in his tracks, when Master James promised to give him a dollar. There certainly was a change come over Master James, when he offered one of his slaves that much money. Solomon commenced to suspect that Aunt Peggy's conjuring had been working mighty strong.

Solomon fetched Master James some clothes and shoes. That same evening Master James appeared at the house, and let on like he just that minute got home from Robinson County. Master Johnson was all ready to talk to him, but Master James sent him away, saying he wasn't feeling very well that night and he would see him tomorrow.

So the next morning after breakfast Master James sent for the overseer and asked him to give him an account of his stewardship. Old Nick told Master James how much work had been done, and got the books and showed him how much money had been saved. Then Master James asked him how had the slaves been behaving, and Master Johnson said they had been good, most of the time, and them that hadn't behaved at first changed their conduct after he got ahold of them, a time or two.

"All except the new slave Mister Dunkin fetched over here, and left on trial while you were gone."

"Tell me all about that new slave. I heard a little about him last night, and it was just too ridiculous. Tell me all about that new slave."

So seeing Master James was good-natured about it, Master Johnson up and told him how he tied up the new hand the first day and gave him forty, because he wouldn't tell him his name.

"Ah ha," said Master James, laughing fit to be killed. "But that's too funny for any use. Tell me some more about that new slave."

So Master Johnson went on and told him how he had to starve the new slave in order to get him to take ahold of a hoe.

"That was the strangest thing for a slave, putting on airs, just like he was a white man! And I reckon you didn't do nothing to him?"

"Oh, no, sir!" said the overseer, grinning like a Cheshire cat, "I didn't do nothing but take the hide off of him."

Master James laughed and laughed, until it appeared like he was just going to bust. "Tell me some more about that new man, oh, tell me some more. That slave interests me, he does, and that's a fact."

Master Johnson didn't quite understand why Master James should make such a great admiration about this slave. But of course he wanted to please the gentleman that hired him, so he explained all about how many times he had to rawhide him, and how he made him do tasks twice as big as some of the other hands, and how he chained him up in the barn at night and fed him on cornbread and water.

"Oh! You're a mighty good overseer; you are the best in the country, Mister Johnson," Master James told him, when his overseer was through with his tale.

"There ain't never been no slave breaker like you around here before. You deserve great credit for sending the slave away before you spoiled him for the market. In fact, you're such a good overseer, and I got this here plantation in such fine shape, that I reckon I don't need you no more. You got the slaves so well trained that I suspect I can run them myself from this time on. But I do wish you had aheld on to that slave until I got home, I would have liked to have seen him, I certainly would've."

The overseer was so astonished he didn't hardly know what to say, but finally he asked Master James if he wouldn't give him a recommendation so he could get another job.

"No, sir," said Master James, "somehow or another I don't like your looks since I've come back this time, and I'd much rather you wouldn't stay around here. In fact, I'm afraid if I was to meet you alone in the woods sometime, I might want to harm you. But laying that aside, I've been looking over these here books of yours, that you kept while I was gone, and for a year or so back. There's some figures that ain't clear to me. I ain't got time to talk about them now, but I expect before I settle with you for the last month you better come up here tomorrow, after I've looked the books and accounts over some more, and then we will straighten the business all up."

Master James allowed afterwards that he was just shooting in the dark when he said that about the books, but howsoever, Master Nick Johnson left that neighborhood between the next two suns, and nobody around here never seen hide nor hair of him since. And all the slaves thanked the Lord, and allowed it was a good riddance of bad rubbish.

But all them things I done told you ain't nothing aside of the changes that came over Master James from that time on. Aunt Peggy's goopher had made a new man of him entirely. The next day after he came back, he told the hands they had to work only from sun to sun, and he cut their tasks down so that nobody had to stand over them with rawhide or a hickory stick. And he let the slaves have a dance in the big barn any Saturday night they wanted to. By and by when Solomon saw how good Master James was, he asked him if he could please send down to the other plantation for his sweetheart. Master James said certainly, and gave Solomon a pass and a note to the overseer on the other plantation, and sent Solomon down to Robinson County with a horse and buggy to fetch his sweetheart back. Soon Miss Libbie heard about the new goings-on at Master James' plantation and she changed her mind about Master James and took him back.

THE GOOPHERED
GRAPEVINE

Old Master Dugal bought this place many years before the war, and I remember well when he set all of this here part of the plantation in scuppernong grapes. The vines grew mighty fast, and Master Dugal made a thousand gallons of scuppernong wine every year.

Now if there's anything a slave likes, it's scuppernong. There ain't nothing that can stand up 'side the scuppernong for sweetness. And when the season is just about over the grapes swell up and the sugar is strong. So I reckon it ain't very astonishing that the slaves liked scuppernong.

It was a sight, all the slaves in the neighborhood sneaking to the vineyard, because Master Dugal had the only vineyard in the neighborhood. Old Master Henry Brayboy's slaves were there, and so were Old Master James McLean's slaves. Even some of the free blacks and poor whites down on Wilmington Road came. I reckon it ain't much nowadays, but before the war, in slavery times, a slave didn't mind going five or ten miles in the night, when there was something good to eat at the other end.

So after a while Master Dugal began to miss his scuppernongs. Of course he accused the slaves of stealing. But we all denied it to the last. Master Dugal set out some spring guns and steel traps. He and the overseer sat up at nights, once or twice, until one night Master Dugal, who was a mighty careless man, got his leg shot full of buckshot. But somehow or another they never caught none of us. I don't know how it happened, but it happened just like I'm telling you and the grapes kept on disappearing just the same.

By and by old Master Dugal fixed up a plan to stop it. There was a conjure woman, Aunt Peggy, living among the free blacks down on Wilmington Road. All the black folks from Rockfish Creek to Beaver Creek were afraid of her. She could work the most powerful kind of goopher. She could make them just dwindle away and die. They say she even went out riding the slaves at night, for she was a witch besides being a conjure woman.

Master Dugal heard about Aunt Peggy's doings and began to reflect whether or not he couldn't get her to help him keep the slaves off the grapevines. One day in the spring of the year, Old Missus packed up a basket of chicken, pound cake, and a bottle of wine. Master Dugal took it in his buggy and drove over to Aunt Peggy's cabin. He took the basket in and had a long talk with her.

The next day Aunt Peggy came up to the vineyard. The slaves saw her slipping around and they soon found out what she was doing. Master Dugal had hired her to goopher the grapevines. She sauntered around among the vines and took a leaf from this one and a grape seed from another one. And then a little twig

from here and a little pinch of dirt from there. She put it all in a big black bottle with a snake's tooth and a speckled hen's egg and some hair from a black cat's tail. Then she filled the bottle with scuppernong wine. When the goopher was all ready and fixed, she took it and went out in the woods and buried it under the root of a red-oak tree. Then she came back and told one of the hands she had goophered the grapevines and any slave who ate any grapes would be sure to die inside of twelve months.

After that the slaves left the scuppernongs alone and Master Dugal didn't have no occasion to find no more fault. The season was almost over when a strange gentleman stopped at the plantation one night to see Master Dugal on some business. His coachman, seeing the scuppernongs growing so nice and sweet, slipped around behind the smokehouse and ate all the scuppernongs he could hold.

Nobody noticed it at the time, but that night on the way home the gentleman's horse ran away and killed the coachman. When we heard the news, Aunt Lucy the cook, she up and said she had seen the strange slave eating the scuppernongs behind the smokehouse. And we knew the goopher had been working. Then one of the black children ran away from the quarters one day, got in the scuppernongs, and died the next week. White folks said he died of the fever, but we knew it was the goopher. So you can see why we didn't have much to do with those vines.

When the scuppernong season was over for that year, Master Dugal found he had made fifteen hundred gallons of wine. One of the slaves heard him laughing with the overseer, saying fifteen hundred gallons of

wine was pretty good interest on ten dollars. So I figured he paid Aunt Peggy ten dollars to goopher the grapevines.

The goopher didn't work no more until next summer when along towards the middle of the season one of the field hands died. That left Master Dugal shorthanded, so he went off to buy another slave. He fetched Henry, a new slave, home with him. He was an old man, the color of gingerbread. But Henry was a pert old man, and he could do a big day's work.

Now it happened that one of the slaves on the next plantation, one of Old Master Henry Brayboy's slaves, had run away the day before, and had taken off for the swamp. Old Master Dugal and some of the other neighboring white folks had gone out with their guns and their dogs to help hunt for the slave. The hands on our own plantation were all so flustered that we forgot to tell the new hand about the goopher on the scuppernong vines. Of course he smelled the grapes and saw the vines. After dark the first thing he did was to slip off to the grapevines, without saying nothing to nobody. The next morning he told the other slaves about the fine scuppernongs he ate the night before.

When they told him about the goopher on the grapevines, he was so terrified that he turned pale and looked just like he was going to die in his tracks. The overseer came up and asked what was the matter. When they told him Henry had been eating the scuppernongs and got the goopher on him, he gave Henry a big drink of whiskey, and allowed that the next raining day he would take him over to Aunt Peggy's and see if she wouldn't take the goopher off of him, seeing as he didn't know nothing about it until he ate the grapes.

Sure enough, it rained the next day, and the over-

seer went over to Aunt Peggy with Henry. Aunt Peggy said being as Henry didn't know about the goopher, and ate the grapes in ignorance of the consequences, she reckoned she might be able to take the goopher off of him. So she fetched out a bottle with some conjuring medicine in it, and poured some out for Henry to drink. He managed to get it down. He said it tasted like whiskey with something bitter in it. She said that it would keep the goopher off of him till spring, but when the sap began to rise in the grapevines, he had better come and see her again, and she would tell him what to do.

Next spring, when the sap commenced to rise in the scuppernong vines, Henry took a ham one night over to Aunt Peggy. She told him that when the master began to prune the grapevines, he must go scrape some of the sap where it oozed out of the cut ends of the vines, and anoint his bald head with it. If he would do that once a year the goopher wouldn't work against him, as long as he did it. Then being as he fetched her the ham, she fixed it so he could eat all the scuppernongs he wanted.

So Henry anointed his head with the sap out of the big grapevines and the goopher never worked against him that summer. But the darndest thing you ever saw happened to Henry. Up to that time he was as bald as a sweet potato, but as soon as the young leaves began to grow out on the grapevines, the hair began to grow out on Henry's head. By the middle of the summer he had the biggest head of hair on the plantation. Before that, Henry had tolerable good hair around the edges. But as soon as the young grapes began to come, Henry's hair began to twirl all up in little balls. By the time the grapes got ripe his head looked just like a bunch of

grapes. Combing it did no good. He would work half the night and would think he had it straightened out, but in the morning the grapes would be there just the same. So he gave it up and tried to keep the grapes down by having his hair cut short.

But that wasn't the queerest thing about the goopher. When Henry came to the plantation, he was getting a little old and stiff in the joints. But that summer he got just as spry and lively as any young man on the plantation. But the most curious thing happened in the fall, when the sap began to go down in the grapevine. First when the grapes were gathered, the knots began to straighten out in Henry's hair. When the leaves began to fall, Henry's hair commenced to drop out. When the vines were bare, Henry's head was balder then it was in the spring. He began to get old in the joints again and paid no more attention to the gals during the whole winter.

Next spring, when he rubbed the sap on again, he get young again and so supple and lively that none of the young slaves could jump, dance, or hoe as much cotton as Henry. But in the fall of the year, his grapes commenced to straighten out and his joints started to get stiff. His hair dropped out. The rheumatism began to wrestle with him.

Now if you knew Old Master Dugal, you would know it had to be a mighty raining day when he couldn't find something for his slaves to do. And it had to be a mighty cloudy night when you could get a dollar by him in the darkness, he could smell money. When he saw how Henry got young in the spring and old in the fall, he allowed to himself as how he could make more money out of Henry than by working him in the cotton field.

68

Well, the next spring, after the sap commenced to rise, and Henry anointed his head and started to get young and supple, Master Dugal took him to town and sold him for fifteen hundred dollars. Of course the man that bought Henry didn't know nothing about the goopher, and Master Dugal didn't see no occasion to tell him. Along toward fall when the sap went down, Henry began to get old again, same as usual. His new master began to get scared, lest he was going to lose his fifteen-hundred-dollar slave. He sent for a mighty fine doctor, but the medicine didn't appear to be no good. The goopher had taken hold. Henry told the doctor about the goopher, but the doctor just laughed it off.

One day in the winter, Master Dugal went to town. He was sauntering along the main street, when who should he meet but Henry's new master. They said, "Howdy," and Master Dugal asked him to have a cigar. After they ran on about the crops and the weather, Master Dugal asked him sort of casual, like as if he just thought of it:

"How do you like the slave I sold you last spring?"

Henry's master shook his head and knocked the ashes off his cigar. "I suspect I made a bad bargain when I bought him. Henry done good work all the summer, but since the fall set in, he appears to be sort of pining away. There ain't nothing particularly the matter with him, leastways the doctor says so, except a touch of rheumatism. But his hair fell out and if he don't pick up his strength mighty soon, I expect I'm going to lose him."

They smoked on a while, and by and by Old Master said, "Well, a bargain's a bargain, but you and me are good friends. I don't want to see you lose all the money you paid for that slave. If what you say is true, and I

expect it is, he ain't worth much now. I guess you worked him too hard this summer. Or else the swamps down here don't agree with a sandhill slave. So you just let me know and if he gets any worse I'll be willing to give you five hundred dollars for him and take my chances on him living."

Sure enough, when Henry began to draw up with the rheumatism and it looked like he was going to die for sure, his new master sent for Master Dugal and Master Dugal gave him what he promised and brought Henry back home. He took good care of him during the winter, gave him whiskey to rub his rheumatism with, and tobacco to smoke, and all he wanted to eat, because a slave that could make a thousand dollars a year don't grow on every huckleberry bush.

Next spring when the sap rose again, Henry's hair commenced to sprout. Master Dugal sold him again down in Robinson County. He kept that selling business up for five years or more. Henry never said nothing about the goopher to his new masters, because he knew he would be taken good care of next winter when Master Dugal bought him back. Master Dugal made enough money off of Henry to buy another plantation over on Beaver Creek.

But along about the end of that fifth year a stranger stopped at the plantation. The first day he was there he and Master Dugal spent all the morning looking over the vineyards. After dinner they spent all the evening playing cards.

The slaves soon discovered that the stranger was a Yankee, and that he came down to North Carolina to learn the white folks how to raise grapes and make wine. He promised Master Dugal he could make the grapevine bear twice as many grapes and that the new

winepress he was selling would make more than twice as many gallons of wine. Old Master Dugal just drank it all in. He appeared to be bewitched by that Yankee.

When the slaves saw that Yankee running around the vineyard and digging under the grapevines, they shook their heads and allowed that they feared Master Dugal was losing his mind. Master Dugal had all the dirt dug away for a week or more. Then that Yankee made the slaves fix up a mixture of lime and ashes and manure and pour it around the roots of the grapevines. Then he advised Master Dugal to trim the vines close. Master Dugal did everything the Yankee told him to do. During all this time, mind you, this here Yankee was living off the fat of the land at the big house. He was playing cards with Master Dugal every night; they say Master Dugal lost more than a thousand dollars during the week that Yankee was a-ruining the grapevines.

When the sap rose next spring, old Henry anointed his head as usual, and his hair commenced to grow the same as it did every year. The scuppernong vines grew mighty fast, and the leaves were greener and thicker than they ever had been. Henry's hair grew out thicker than ever, and he appeared to get younger and younger, suppler and suppler. Since he was short of hands that spring, having taken in considerable new ground, Master Dugal concluded he wouldn't sell Henry until he got the crop in the cotton shop, so he kept Henry on the plantation.

But along about the time for the grapes to come on the scuppernong vines, there appeared to come a change over them. The leaves withered and shriveled up. The young grapes turned yellow and by and by everybody on the plantation could see that the whole

vineyard was dying. Master Dugal took water to the vines and did what he could, but it wasn't any use. That Yankee had burst the watermelon. One time the vines picked up a little bit, and Master Dugal allowed they were going to come out again. But that Yankee had dug too close to the vines and all that lime and ashes had burnt the life out of them, and they just kept a-withering and shriveling.

All this time the goopher was a-working. When the vines started to wither, Henry commenced to complain about his rheumatism. When the leaves began to dry up, his hair commenced to drop out. When the vines freshened up a little bit, Henry would get pert again, and when the vines withered again, Henry would get old again. He just kept getting more and more fit for nothing. He just pined away. Finally he took to his cabin. When the vine where he got the sap to anoint his head withered and turned yellow and died, Henry died too. He just went out sort of like a candle. There didn't seem to be nothing the matter with him, except the rheumatism. His strength just dwindled away until he didn't have enough left to draw his breath. We knew that the goopher had reached out and got Henry for good.

HOT-FOOT HANNIBAL

Chloe used to belong to Old Master Dugal. She was a likely woman and smart. The Old Missus brought her up to the big house and taught her the ways of white folks. By and by she became the missus' personal maid, and began to think she ran the house herself, to hear her talk about it.

Well, one time Master Dugal wanted a houseboy. He sent down to the quarters to have Jeff and Hannibal come up to the big house next morning. Old Master and Old Missus looked the two boys over and discussed with themselves for a little while, and then Master Dugal said:

"We like Hannibal the best and we're going to keep him. Hannibal, you'll work at the house from now on. And if you're a good slave and mind your business, I'll give you Chloe for a wife next spring. You other slave, you Jeff, you can go back to the quarters. We ain't going to need you."

Now Chloe had been standing there behind Old Missus during all this here talk. Chloe had made up her mind from the very first minute she set eyes on the

two, that she didn't like Hannibal and she was never
going to like him. On the other hand she was sure she
liked Jeff, regardless if Master Dugal chose him to work
at the big house. Of course Chloe was mighty sorry
when Old Master chose Hannibal and sent Jeff back.
So she slipped around the house and caught Jeff on his
way back to the quarters. She told him not to be down-
hearted, she was going to see if she couldn't find some
way or another to get rid of Hannibal and get Jeff up
to the house in his place.

The new houseboy caught on mighty fast, and it
wasn't no time before Master Dugal and Old Missus
thought Hannibal was the best houseboy they had ever
had. But Chloe didn't like his ways. He was so sure he
was going to have her in the spring that he didn't appear to figure he had to do any courting.

When he ran across her about the house, he would
swell up in a biggity way and say, "Come here and kiss
me, honey. You're going to be mine in the spring.
You're not acting as fond of me as you ought to be."

The more familiar Hannibal got, the more Chloe
thought about Jeff. So one evening she went down to
the quarters and waited until she had a chance to talk
to Jeff by himself. She told him to go down and see
Aunt Peggy, the conjure woman, and ask her to give
him something to help get Hannibal out of the big
house. And being that Jeff didn't have nothing to give
Aunt Peggy, Chloe gave him a silver dollar and a silk
handkerchief to pay with. Aunt Peggy never liked to
work for nobody for nothing.

Jeff slipped off down to Aunt Peggy's one night.
He gave her the present he brought, and told her all
about him and Chloe and Hannibal. He asked her to
help him out. Aunt Peggy told him she would work

her roots and for him to come back the next night, and she would tell him what she could do for him.

The next night Jeff went back and Aunt Peggy gave him a baby doll, with a body made out of a piece of cornstalk and splinters for arms and legs. The head was made out of an elderberry pit, and it had two little red peppers for feet.

"This here baby doll," said Aunt Peggy, "is Hannibal. This pit head is Hannibal's head, and these pepper feet are Hannibal's feet. You take this and hide it under the house on the beam under the door where he will have to walk over it every day. And as long as Hannibal comes anywhere near this baby doll, he'll be just like it is—light-headed and hot-footed. If them two things don't get him in trouble mighty soon, I'm not a conjure woman. But when you get Hannibal out of the house and get all through with this baby doll, you must bring it back to me, because it's a mighty powerful goopher, and it could make more trouble if you leave it lying around."

Well, Jeff took the baby doll and slipped up to the big house and whistled to Chloe, and when she came out he told her what old Aunt Peggy had said. And Chloe showed him how to get under the house, and when he had put the conjure doll on the beam, he went back to the quarters.

The next day, sure enough, the goopher started to work. Hannibal started in the house with an armful of wood to make a fire. He had no more got across the door before his feet started to burn so that he dropped the wood on the floor and woke the missus up a hour sooner than usual. Of course the missus didn't like that and spoke sharp about it.

When dinnertime came, Hannibal was helping the

cook bring the dinner from the kitchen into the big house. In those days the kitchen was a room behind the house. As Hannibal was getting close to the door where he had to go in, his feet started to burn and his head began to swim. He dropped a big plate of chicken and dumplings down in the dirt in the middle of the yard. The white folks had to make their dinner off of cold ham and sweet potatoes.

The next day he overslept and got into more trouble. After breakfast, Master Dugal sent him over to Master Marlboro to borrow a monkey wrench. He should have been back in a half an hour, but he came poking home about dinnertime with a screwdriver instead of a monkey wrench. Master Dugal had to send another slave back with the screwdriver, and Hannibal didn't get no dinner. That afternoon, Hannibal was told to weed the flowers in the front garden, and he dug up all the bulbs the missus had sent away for and had paid alot of money for. He took them down to the hog pen and fed them to the hogs. When the Old Missus came out in the cool of the evening and saw what Hannibal had done, she was almost crazy, and she wrote a note and sent Hannibal down to the overseer with it.

But the whipping Hannibal got from the overseer didn't appear to do any good. Every now and then his feet started to torment him and his mind would get all mixed up. His conduct got worse, until finally the white folks couldn't stand it anymore, and they sent Hannibal back to the quarters.

"Mister Smith," said Master Dugal to the overseer, "this here slave has gotten so trifling here lately that we can't keep him at the house no more. I fetched him to you to be straightened up. You've had occasion to

deal with him once, so he knows what to expect. You just take him in hand, and let me know how he turns out. When the hands come in from the field this evening, you can send that yellow slave Jeff up to the house. I'll try him and see if he's any better than Hannibal."

So Jeff went up to the big house and pleased Master Dugal and Old Missus so well that they all got to liking him, and they forgot about Hannibal. Chloe and Jeff were so interested in each other since Jeff came to the big house that they forgot all about taking the baby doll back to Aunt Peggy, and it kept working for a while, and making Hannibal's feet burn more or less, until everyone on the plantation got to calling him Hot-Foot Hannibal. He kept getting more and more trifling, until he got the name of being the worst slave on the plantation. Master Dugal threatened to sell him in the spring. Finally the goopher quit working, and Hannibal started to pick up.

Now Hannibal wasn't dumb, and when rid of them sore feet, his mind kept running on his other troubles. Three or four weeks before he had had an easy job, waiting on the white folks, living off the fat of the land and promised the finest woman on the plantation for a wife. And now here he was back in the cotton field with the overseer cursing him, with nothing to eat but cornbread, bacon, and molasses. All the field hands were making fun of him because he had been sent back from the big house to the field. The more Hannibal thought about it the madder he got, until he finally swore he was going to get even with Jeff and Chloe, if it was the last thing he did.

So Hannibal slipped away from the quarters one

Sunday and hid in the cotton close to the big house, until he saw Chloe going down the road.

"Howdy, Chloe," he said.

"I ain't got no time to fool with a field hand," said Chloe, tossing her head. "What you want with me, Hot-Foot?"

"I want to know how you and Jeff are getting along."

"I don't think that's any of your business. I don't see what occasion any common field hand has got to mix in with the affairs of folks who live in the big house. But if it'll do you any good to know, I might say that me and Jeff are getting along mighty well, and we're going to get married in the spring. And you won't be invited to the wedding, neither!"

"No, no," he said, "I wouldn't expect to be invited to the wedding, being a common, low-down field hand like I am. But I'm glad to hear you and Jeff are getting along so well. I thought he might be getting a little tired."

"Tired of me? That's ridiculous!" said Chloe. "Why, that man loves me so, I believe he would go through fire and water for me."

"I see," said Hannibal. "Then I reckon it must be someone else who meets a woman down by the creek every Sunday evening, to say nothing about two or three times a week."

"Yes, it must be, and you're a liar if you say it's Jeff."

"Maybe I'm a liar, and maybe I don't have good eyes. But unless I'm a liar, or unless I don't have good eyes, Jeff is going to meet that woman this evening about eight o'clock down there by the creek."

Well, Chloe told Hannibal she didn't believe a word he said, and called him a low-down liar, who was trying to slander Jeff because he was luckier than he was. But she couldn't keep her mind from running on about what Hannibal had said. She remembered she had heard one of the other slaves say there was a woman over on the next plantation that Jeff used to go with, before he became acquainted with Chloe. Then she started remembering other little things that she had taken no notice of before, and what would make it appear like Jeff had something on his mind.

Chloe was very much in love with Jeff, and would have done almost anything for him, as long as he stuck by her. But Chloe was a mighty jealous woman, and while she didn't believe what Hannibal said, she saw how it could have been so, so she decided to find out for herself.

Now, Chloe hadn't seen Jeff all day, because the master had sent him over to another plantation to do some work. Jeff wasn't expected home until evening. But just after supper was over, and while the ladies were sitting out on the patio, Chloe slipped off from the house and ran down the road, to the creek, and hid in the bushes. Sure enough she saw Jeff sitting on the bank under a willow tree. Every now and then he would get up and look up the road.

First Chloe felt like she would go right over and give Jeff a piece of her mind. Then she figured she better wait and be sure before she did anything. So she waited, all the time getting madder and madder. Finally she saw a woman coming down the road. And when she saw Jeff jump up and run towards that woman, and throw his arms around her neck, poor

Chloe didn't stop to see no more, but just turned around and ran up to the house and told Master Dugal and Old Missus all about the baby doll, and all about Jeff getting the goopher from Aunt Peggy, and about what the goopher had done to Hannibal.

Master Dugal was mighty mad. He didn't let on at first like he believed Chloe, but when she took him and showed him where to find the baby doll, Master Dugal turned white as chalk.

"What devil's work is this," said he. "No wonder poor Hannibal's feet ached. Something's got to be done to teach that old witch to keep her hands off my slaves. And as for Jeff, I'm going to do just what I told all my slaves I would do, if I found out they were using conjuring."

Master Dugal had warned the hands before about fooling with conjuring. The fact was, he had lost one or two slaves himself from them being goophered, and he would have had old Aunt Peggy whipped long ago, only she was a free woman, and he was afraid she would conjure him. Although Master Dugal said he didn't believe in conjuring and such, he decided to be on the safe side and let Aunt Peggy alone. But he did what he said he was going to do with Jeff. He sold him the next day to a speculator, who started down the river with him the next morning on a steamboat for Alabama.

Now when Chloe told Old Master Dugal about the baby doll, she didn't think he would sell Jeff down south. However, she was so mad with Jeff that she persuaded herself she didn't care, and so she held her head up and went around looking like she was real glad about it.

Then one day she met Hannibal. And when he saw her, he just busted out laughing.

"What you laughing at, Hot-Foot?" she demanded.

Hannibal kept on laughing until finally he said, "I'm laughing at how I made a fool of you."

Chloe turned pale and her heart came up in her mouth. "What do you mean?" she said, catching ahold of a bush by the road to steady herself. "What do you mean when you said you fooled me?"

"What do I mean? I mean that I got squared up with you for treating me the way you did, and I got even with Jeff for cutting me out. Now he's going to know what it's like to eat cornbread and molasses once more, and work from daylight to dark, to have an overseer driving him from one day to the next. I mean that I sent word to Jeff that Sunday that you wanted to meet him down by the creek. Then I put on a frock and a sunbonnet and fixed myself up to look like a woman. When Jeff saw me coming he ran up to meet me, thinking I was you, and you saw him, and that's what you saw. Now I reckon you and Jeff both know what it means to mess with me."

Poor Chloe hadn't heard more than half of the last part of what Hannibal said, but she had heard enough to learn that she had been tricked. And her Jeff hadn't done anything. For loving her too much and going to meet her, she had caused him to be sold away, where she would never, never see him no more.

Hannibal hadn't no more than finished what he had to say when Chloe's knees gave away under her, and she fell down in the road and laid there half an hour or so before she came to. When she did, she crept up to the big house just as pale as a ghost. And for a month or so she crawled around the house and ap-

peared to be so poorly that Master Dugal sent for a doctor, and the doctor kept on asking her questions until he found she was just pining away for Jeff.

When he told Master Dugal, he just laughed and said he'd fix that. She could have the new houseboy for a husband. But Old Missus said no, Chloe ain't that kind of person, and that Master Dugal should buy Jeff back.

So he wrote a letter to the speculator saying he would like to buy Jeff back again. Chloe started to pick up a little when Old Missus told her about this letter. However, Master Dugal got an answer from the speculator, saying he was mighty sorry, but Jeff had fallen overboard or jumped off the steamboat and had drowned.

When Chloe heard this she wasn't much use to anyone. She pretended to do her work, and Old Missus put up with her, and had the doctor give her medicine, and let her go to the circus, and all sorts of things, to take her mind off of her troubles. But they didn't do any good. Chloe got to slipping down to the creek at nights, just like she was coming to meet Jeff. And she would sit under the willow tree and wait for him, night after night. Until she got so bad the white folks sent her over to their daughter to give her a change. But she ran away the first night, and when they looked for her the next morning, they found her corpse lying under the willow tree.

Every since then, Chloe's haint comes every evening and sits down under that willow tree and waits for Jeff, or else walks up and down the road looking and looking. Waiting and waiting for her sweetheart that ain't never, never coming back to her.

SISTER BECKY'S CHILD

Becky used to belong to Old Colonel Penleton, who owned a plantation down on Wilmington Road, about ten miles from here, just before you get to Black Swamp. Becky was a field hand, and a mighty good one. She had a husband once, a slave from the next plantation. But the man who owned her husband died and his land and slaves had to be sold to pay his debts. Colonel Penleton had bought this slave, but soon after, he had been betting on horse races, and didn't have any money, so Becky's husband was sold away.

Of course Becky went on some about losing her man, but she couldn't help herself, and besides that, she had her son to comfort her. This here little Mose was the cutest, blackest, shiniest-eye baby you ever laid eyes on. He was as fond of his mother as his mother was of him. Of course Becky had to work and didn't have much time to spend with her child. Old Aunt Nancy, the plantation nurse down in the quarters, used to take care of little Mose in the daytime, and after the slaves came in from the cotton field Becky would take her child and kiss him, and nurse him, and keep

him until morning. On Sundays she would have him in her cabin with her all day long.

Sister Becky had gotten sort of used to getting along without her husband, when one day Colonel Penleton went to the races. Of course when he went to the races, he took his horses, and of course he bet on his own horses and of course he lost his money. Colonel Penleton didn't never have no luck with his horses.

There was a horse named Lightning Bug, that belonged to another man, and the horse won the sweepstakes. Colonel Penleton took to liking that horse, and asked his owner what he was willing to take for him.

"I'll take a thousand dollars for that horse," said this here man, who had a big plantation down towards Wilmington Road where he raised horses to race and sell.

Well, Colonel Penleton scratched his head and wondered where he was going to raise a thousand dollars. He didn't see how he could do it, because he owed as much as he could borrow already on the security he could give. But he was just bound to have that horse. So said he, "I'll give you my note for eleven hundred dollars for that horse."

The other man shook his head and said, "Your note is better than gold, I don't doubt. But I made it a rule in my business not to take no notes from nobody. However, sir, if you got your mind set on that horse, most likely we can make some kind of bargain. And while we're talking, I might as well say that I need another slave down on my place. If you got a good one to spare, I might trade with you."

Now the Colonel didn't really have no slave to spare, but he told himself it was the best thing to have that horse, and so he said: "Well, I don't like to, but

I reckon I'll have to. You come out to my plantation tomorrow and look over my slaves, and pick out the one you want."

Sure enough, the next day this here man came out to Colonel Penleton's place and rode around the plantation and glanced at the slaves, and who should he pick out, out of all of them, but Sister Becky.

"I need a new slave woman down to my place," he said, "to cook and wash and so on. That young woman will just fill the bill. You give me her, and you can have Lightning Bug."

Now Colonel Penleton didn't like to trade Sister Becky, because she was just about the best field hand he had. And besides, he didn't care to take the mothers away from their children while they were still young. But this man said he wanted Becky, or else Colonel Penleton couldn't have the racehorse.

"Well," said the Colonel, "you can have the woman. But I don't like to send her away from her baby. What you going to give me for that slave child?"

"I don't want the baby. I ain't got no use for the baby."

"I tell you what I'll do, I'll throw that child in for good measure."

But the other man shook his head. "No, sir, I'd be much obliged, but I don't raise slaves. I raise horses. I don't want to be bothered with no babies. Never mind the child. I'll keep that woman so busy she'll forget the baby. Slaves are made to work, and they ain't got time for such foolishness as babies."

Colonel Penleton didn't want to hurt Becky's feelings, because he was a kindhearted man, and never liked to make trouble for nobody. So he told Becky he was going to send her down to Robinson County for

a day or so, to help out his son-in-law in his work. And being this other man was going that way, he had asked him to take her along in his buggy.

"Can I carry little Mose with me, Master?" asked Sister Becky.

"No," said the Colonel, as if he was thinking whether to let her take him or not, "I reckon you better let Aunt Nancy look after your baby for the day or two you'll be gone and she'll see that he gets enough to eat until you get back."

So Sister Becky hugged and kissed little Mose, and told him to be good, and take care of himself and not to forget his mother while she was gone. Little Mose put his arms around his mother and laughed and smiled just like it was mighty fine for his mother to go away and leave him.

Well, this here horse trader started out with Becky, and by and by after they had gone down the road for a few miles or so, this man turned around in a different direction and kept going that a-way until by and by Sister Becky up and asked him if he was going to Robinson County by a new road.

"No," he said. "I ain't going to Robinson County at all. I'm going to Bladen County, where my planta-tion is, and where I raise horses."

"But how am I going to get to Miss Laura's planta-tion down in Robinson County?" she asked, with her heart in her mouth, for she commenced to get scared all of a sudden.

"You ain't going to get there at all," said the man. "You belong to me now. I traded my best racehorse for you. If you are a good gal, I'll treat you right, and if you don't behave yourself, why, what happens will be your own fault."

Of course Sister Becky cried and went on about her baby. But of course it didn't do no good, and by and by they got down to this here man's place, and he put Sister Becky to work, and forgot all about her having a child.

Meanwhile, when evening came that same day, little Mose commenced to get restless. By and by, when his mother didn't come, he started to cry for her. Aunt Nancy fed him and rocked him, and finally he just cried and cried until he cried himself to sleep.

The next day he didn't appear to be as pert as usual, and when night came he fretted and went on worse than he did the night before. The next day his little eyes started to lose their shine, and he wouldn't eat. He started to look so peaked that Aunt Nancy took and carried him up to the big house, and showed him to her Old Missus. The Old Missus gave her some medicine for him, and said if he didn't get better she should fetch him up to the big house again, and they would get a doctor, and nurse little Mose up there.

But Aunt Nancy had learned to like little Mose, and she didn't want to have him up at the big house. And so when he didn't get any better she gathered a mess of green peas, and took the peas and the baby to see old Aunt Peggy, the conjure woman. She gave Aunt Peggy the mess of peas, and told her all about Sister Becky and little Mose.

"That is a mighty small mess of peas you brought up here," said Aunt Peggy.

"Yes, I know," said Aunt Nancy. "But this here is a mighty small baby."

"You will have to fetch me something more," said Aunt Peggy. "For you can't expect me to waste my time digging roots and working conjuring for nothing."

"All right, I'll fetch you something more next time."

"You better," said Aunt Peggy, "or else there will be trouble. What this here child needs is to see his mother. You leave him here until evening and I'll show him his mother."

So when Aunt Nancy had gone away, Aunt Peggy took and worked her roots, and turned little Mose to a hummingbird, and sent him off to find his mother.

Little Mose flew and flew and flew away, until by and by he got to the place where Sister Becky belonged. He saw his mother working around the yard, and he could tell from looking at her that she was troubled in her mind about something and feeling kind of poorly. Sister Becky heard something humming around and around her, sweet and low. First she thought it was a hummingbird; then she thought it sounded like her little Mose crooning on her breast. She just imagined it was her little Mose, and it made her feel better.

She went on about her work perter than she had done since she had been down there. Little Mose stayed around until late in the evening, then he flew back as hard as he could to Aunt Peggy. Sister Becky dreamed that night that she was holding her child in her arms, and kissing him and nursing him, just like she used to do back on the old plantation where he was born. For three or four days Sister Becky went about her work with more spirit than she had shown since she had been down here at this man's plantation.

The next day, after he came back, little Mose was more pert and better than he had been for a long time. But towards the end of the week he commenced to get restless again, and stopped eating, and Aunt Nancy carried him down to Aunt Peggy once more, and she

turned him to a mockingbird this time, and sent him off to see his mother again.

It didn't take him long to get there, and when he did he saw her standing in the kitchen looking back in the direction little Mose was coming from. There were tears in her eyes, and she looked more poorly and peaked than she had when he was down there before. So little Mose set on a tree in the yard and sung, and sung, and sung, just fitting to split his throat. First Sister Becky didn't notice him, but this mockingbird kept staying around the house all day, and by and by Sister Becky just imagined that mockingbird was her little Mose's crooning and crooning, just like he used to when she would come home at night from the cotton field. The mockingbird stayed around there most of the day, and when Sister Becky went out in the yard one time, this mockingbird lit on her shoulder and pecked at a piece of bread she was eating. He fluttered his wings so as to rub up against the side of her head. When he flew away late in the evening, just before sundown, Sister Becky felt better than she had since she had heard that hummingbird a week or so before. That night she dreamed about old times again.

But this here carrying little Mose down to old Aunt Peggy, and this here getting things for to pay her used up a lot of Aunt Nancy's time, and she began to get kind of tired. Besides that, when Sister Becky had been on the plantation, she had helped Aunt Nancy with the young ones in the evenings and on Sundays. And Aunt Nancy started to miss her mighty bad, especially since she had a touch of rheumatism herself. So she said to Aunt Peggy one day: "Isn't there no way you can fetch Sister Becky home?"

"I don't know about that. I'll have to work my

roots and find out whether I can or not. But it'll take a mighty heap of work and I can't waste my time for nothing. If you'll fetch me something to pay me for my trouble, I reckon we can fix it."

So the next day Aunt Nancy went down to see the conjure woman again and brought her best Sunday head-handkerchief, and Aunt Peggy looked at the head-handkerchief, ran her hand over it, and said, "Yes, that will do fine. I've been working my roots since you have been gone. I think that most likely I can get Sister Becky back, but it's going to take figuring and studying as well as conjuring. The first thing to do is to stop fetching that baby down here, and not send him to see his mother no more. If he gets too poorly, you let me know, and I'll make him forget Sister Becky for a week or so. So unless you come for that, you need not come back to see me no more, until I send for you."

So Aunt Peggy sent Aunt Nancy away, and the first thing she did was to call a hornet from a nest. "You go up to Colonel Penleton's stable, hornet," she said, "and sting the knees of the racehorse named Lightning Bug. Be sure to get the right one."

So the hornet flew up to Colonel Penleton's stables and stung Lightning Bug around the legs, and the next morning Lightning Bug's knees were all swollen up, twice as big as they should be. When Colonel Penleton went out to the stable and saw the horse's legs, it would've made you tremble like a leaf to hear him curse that horse trader. However, he cooled off and told the stable boy to rub Lightning Bug's legs with some liniment. The next day the swelling had gone down, considerable. Aunt Peggy had sent a sparrow, that had a nest in one of the trees close to her cabin, to watch what was going on around the big

house, and when this here sparrow told her the horse was getting over the swelling, she sent the hornet back to sting his knees some more, and the next morning Lightning Bug's legs were swollen up worse than before.

Well, this time Colonel Penleton was mad through and through, and he really cursed that horse trader. He went right to the house and got out his pen and ink, and wrote a letter saying:

"You have sold me a horse which has got a ring-bone, or a sprain, or something, and I paid you for a sound horse. I want you to send my slave woman back and take your old horse or else I'll sue you, sure as you're born!"

But this here man wasn't scared a bit, and he wrote back that a bargain was a bargain. That Lightning Bug was sound when he sold him, and if the Colonel didn't know enough about horses to take care of a fine racer, that was his own fault. He said the Colonel could sue and curse all he wanted, but he wasn't going to give up Sister Becky.

Aunt Peggy knew what was going on, all this time, and fixed up a little bag with some roots and one thing or another in it, and gave it to this sparrow and had him take it to where Sister Becky was. The sparrow dropped it right in front of Becky's cabin, where she would be sure to find it, the first time she came out the door.

So that night Sister Becky dreamed her child was dead, and the next day she was moaning and groaning all day. She dreamed three nights running, and then, the next morning after the last dream, she found this here little bag and she figured she had been conjured and was going to die.

Her master laughed at her, and argued with her, and tried to persuade her out of her fool notion, as he called it, because he was one of these here white folks that pretended they didn't believe in conjuring. But it was no use. Sister Becky kept getting worse and worse, until finally this here man thought she was going to die sure enough. And as he knew there had to be nothing the matter with Lightning Bug when he traded him, he figured maybe he could fix him up, at least good enough to sell again. Anyhow, a lame horse was better than a dead slave. So he sat down and wrote Colonel Penleton a letter:

"My conscience has been troubling me about that ringbone horse I sold you. Some folks think a horse trader ain't got no conscience, but they don't know me, for that's my weakness, and the reason I ain't made no more money horse-trading. The fact is, I've got so I can't sleep a night from worrying about that sprain horse. And I made up my mind that while a bargain is a bargain, and you saw Lightning Bug before you traded for him, principle is worth more than money, horses, or even slaves. So if you'll send Lightning Bug down here, I'll send your slave woman back, and we'll call the trade off, and be as good friends as we ever were, with no hard feelings."

The Colonel sent his horse back. When the man that brought the horse back told Sister Becky that her baby wasn't dead, she was so glad that she figured she was going to try to live until she got back where she could see little Mose once more. When she reached the old plantation and saw her baby kicking, and crooning, and holding out his arms towards her, she wished she wasn't conjured and didn't have to die. When Aunt Nancy told her all about the conjure woman,

Sister Becky went down to see her. Then the conjure woman took the goopher off her, and she got well and stayed on the plantation, and raised her baby. When little Mose grew up he could sing and whistle just like a mockingbird, so that the white folks used to have him come up to the big house at night, and whistle and sing for them, and they used to give him money and food and one thing or another, which he always took home to his mother, because he knew what she had gone through. He turned out to be a smart man and learned the blacksmith trade. The Colonel let him hire his time. By and by he bought his mother and set her free. And then he bought himself and took care of Sister Becky as long as they both lived.

RAY ANTHONY SHEPARD was born in Sedalia, Missouri, and grew up in Lincoln, Nebraska. He received a bachelor's degree from the University of Nebraska and his master's in education from Harvard, where he was a Martin Luther King fellow. He is now a doctoral candidate at Harvard and also a full-time editor of a reading program in New York. *Sneakers,* Mr. Shepard's first book, was a Council on Interracial Books for Children award-winner. He is married and has two children.

JOHN ROSS and CLARE ROMANO are well-known artists who work individually and as a husband-and-wife team. They both studied at Cooper Union School of Art in New York. John Ross is chairman of Manhattanville College's art department and Clare Romano is a professor at Pratt Institute. Their prints are in numerous museum and university collections. Recently they co-authored a definitive work on printmaking.

The illustrations in *Conjure Tales* were done in collagraphs, a new intaglio technique that is essentially a printed collage of various materials. The plates prepared by the artists were made by adhering these materials to cardboard with acrylics, inked as traditional etchings, and printed on Arches etching paper in an etching press.

The text type is set in Baskerville and the display type in Neuland. The book is printed by offset at Halliday Lithograph.